W9-BLJ-008

For Mom
—D. C.

To Claire Rose Reilly
and Logan Patrick McMurray
—B. L.

No part of this publication may be reproduced, stored in a retrieval system, or transmitted in any form or by any means, electronic, mechanical, photocopying, recording, or otherwise, without written permission of the publisher. For information regarding permission, write to Atheneum Books for Young Readers, an imprint of Simon & Schuster Children's Publishing Division, 1230 Avenue of the Americas, New York, NY 10020.

ISBN-13: 978-0-545-11011-2
ISBN-10: 0-545-11011-4

Text copyright © 2006 by Doreen Cronin.
Illustrations copyright © 2006 by Betsy Lewin.
All rights reserved. Published by Scholastic Inc.,
557 Broadway, New York, NY 10012, by arrangement
with Atheneum Books for Young Readers, an imprint of
Simon & Schuster Children's Publishing Division.
SCHOLASTIC and associated logos are trademarks
and/or registered trademarks of Scholastic Inc.

12 11 10 9 8 7 6 5 4 3 2   8 9 10 11 12 13/0

Printed in the U.S.A.   40

First Scholastic printing, October 2008

Book design by Ann Bobco

The text for this book is set in Filosofia.

The illustrations for this book are rendered
in brush and watercolor.

Dooby Dooby Moo

by
doreen cronin
and
betsy lewin

SCHOLASTIC INC.
New York Toronto London Auckland Sydney
Mexico City New Delhi Hong Kong Buenos Aires

Farmer Brown keeps a very close eye on his animals. Every night he listens outside the barn door.

Dooby, dooby moo . . .
the cows snore.

Fa la, la, la baaaa . . .
the sheep snore.

Whacka, whacka quack . . .
Duck snores.

Duck keeps a very close eye
on Farmer Brown.

Every morning Duck borrows
his newspaper. One day,
an ad catches his eye:

TALENT SHOW!!!

OPEN TO ALL!!

where: COUNTY FAIR
when: SATURDAY

1st prize: **A TRAMPOLINE!!***

2nd prize: **BOX OF CHALK****

3rd prize: **VEGGIE CHOP-O-MATIC**

* Slightly used. Sponsor makes no warranty, expressed or implied, nor assumes any responsibility in the use of the trampoline.

** Actual amount awarded will be based on availability.

As soon as Farmer Brown opened his paper, he knew the animals were up to something.

Farmer Brown watched them closely all day.

He watched them
from above.

He watched them from below.

He even watched them upside down.

Outside the barn, late at night, he heard,

Dooby, dooby moo . . .
Fa la, la, la baaaa . . .
Whacka, whacka QUack . . .

Inside the barn, the cows rehearsed "Twinkle, Twinkle, Little Star."

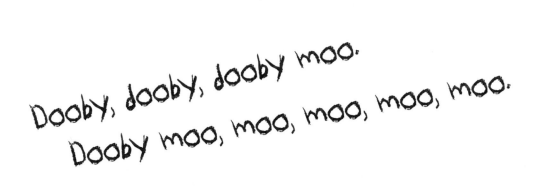

Dooby, dooby, dooby moo.
Dooby moo, moo, moo, moo, moo.

Needs work, Duck noted.

The sheep rehearsed
"Home on the Range."

Baaa, baaa, baaa, baaabaaa.
Fa la baaa, fa la baaaa, baaaabaaabaaa!

Duck had them try it again,
with more feeling.

The pigs did an interpretive dance.

whacka, whacka
Quaaack . . .

snored Duck.

Day after day, Farmer Brown kept a very close eye on the animals.

He watched from the left.

He watched from the right.

He even watched in disguise.

Outside the barn, night after night, he heard:

Dooby, dooby moo . . .

Fa la, la, la baaaa . . .

Whacka, whacka quack . . .

**Inside the barn, night after night,
the animals rehearsed.**

Finally it was time for the county fair.

Duck was
pacing
back
and forth.

The pigs were combing their hair.

The cows were drinking tea with lemon.

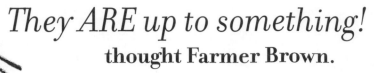

They ARE up to something!
thought Farmer Brown.

**Farmer Brown
was not going
to leave them alone.**

He loaded all the animals into the

back of his truck and drove to the fair.

When he got there he heard:

Dooby, dooby moo . . .

Fa la, la, la baaaa . . .

Whacka, whacka QUACK . . .

He parked his truck and headed off to
the free barbecue.

When Farmer Brown was out of sight, the animals ran to the talent show desk and signed in.*

Cows
Sheep
Pigs

* Contestants consent to the use of his/her name, photograph, and/or likeness for advertising and promotional purposes in connection with this promotion without additional compensation, unless prohibited by law.

The cows sang
"Twinkle, Twinkle, Little Star."

Dooby, dooby, dooby moo.

Dooby moo, moo, moo, moo, moo, moo.

Two of the judges were clearly impressed.

The sheep sang "Home on the Range."

la, la baa.

ba, ba, baaa, baa, ba, baaaa.

Three of the judges were clearly impressed.

It was time for the pigs' interpretive dance.
But they were sound asleep.

Shloink oink, oink, oink, oink.

All of the judges were clearly annoyed.

Duck really wanted that trampoline.
He jumped on stage and sang
"Born to Be Wild."*

QUack, QUack, QUUUaaaaaaCKK!

The judges gave him a standing ovation.

* Original words and music by Mars Bonfire

When Farmer Brown got back to the truck,
   he heard:

Dooby, dooby moo . . .
   Fa la, la, la baaaa . . .
      Whacka, whacka QUack . . .

The animals were exactly where he had
   left them.

That night Farmer Brown listened outside the barn door.

Dooby, dooby BOING!

Fa la, la, la BOING!

Whacka, whacka BOING!

The events and characters depicted in this picture book are fictitious.
Any similarity to actual persons, living or otherwise, is purely coincidental.